THE MENINO

ISOL

Text and illustrations copyright © 2015 by Isol
Translation copyright © 2015 by Elisa Amado
Published in Canada and the USA in 2015 by Groundwood Books

Groundwood Books / House of Anansi Press
110 Spadina Avenue, Suite 801, Toronto, Ontario M5V 2K4
or c/o Publishers Group West
1700 Fourth Street, Berkeley, CA 94710

We acknowledge for their financial support of our publishing
program the Government of Canada through the Canada Book Fund
(CBF).

Library and Archives Canada Cataloguing in Publication
Isol
[Menino. English]
The menino / written and illustrated by Isol ; translated by Elisa
Amado.
Translation of: El menino.
Issued in print and electronic formats.
ISBN 978-1-55498-778-8 (bound).—ISBN 978-1-55498-779-5 (pdf)
I. Amado, Elisa, translator II. Title. III. Title: Menino. English.
PZ7.I86Me 2015   j863'.64   C2015-900030-0
C2015-900031-9

The illustrations are in pencil and pen on paper, and Photoshop.
Design by Michael Solomon
Printed and bound in Malaysia

MIX
Paper from
responsible sources
FSC® C012700
www.fsc.org

32013 6813

Dedicated to Anton
and his father

Translated by Elisa Amado

Groundwood Books
House of Anansi Press
Toronto Berkeley

THE MENINO
A STORY BASED ON
REAL EVENTS

ISOL

The house is peaceful.
The neighborhood, silent.
The cat, asleep.
The people, busy with their own things.

Days follow one another in an orderly way.
After Tuesday, comes Wednesday...

until the Menino arrives.

"Catch him. He mustn't fall!" yells the mother.

"I've got him! I've got him!" quakes the father.

The Menino arrives
naked and yelling,
as if to make sure
everyone notices.

And everyone does notice.

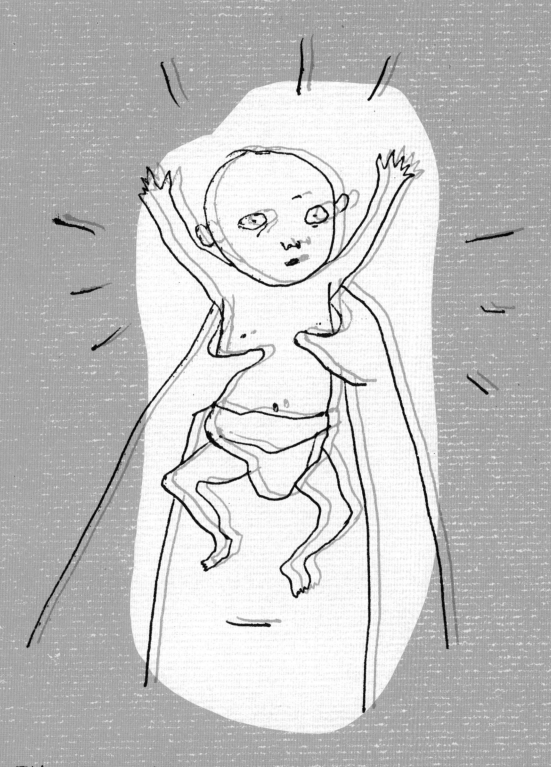

It's a big deal!
Where does he come from? Where was he before?
Does he look like us?

The Menino
has been on a long voyage
and needs to sleep.

It's easy
to make room for him,
he is so small.

Did the Menino know where he was going
when his voyage began?
Or did he arrive at this house by chance?

Why does he move as though he were swimming
through the air?
Is he still dreaming?

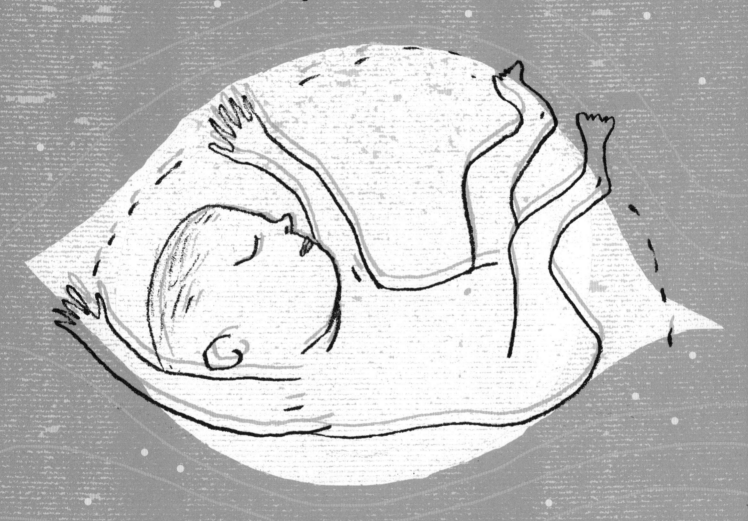

The new arrival doesn't seem to know yet
how to use his earthly body's commands.
He can't see too well. He is just learning to breathe...

A good host will lend him a hand.

This siren is activated when you must
feed the Menino,
put the Menino to sleep,
clean the Menino,
play with the Menino,
hug the Menino.

It's fun trying to guess the
right thing to do each time.

The Menino arrives
very hungry
and has to eat often.

He activates a pump
that he has in his mouth
and uses it to sip
and suck.

He prefers the milk
that is prepared by the woman of the house.

The Menino has two little windows up high
that he uses to see what's going on outside.

To rest, he lowers the curtains.
Then he can only see inside.

If the Menino feels bad for any reason,
he makes salty water spring forth
through these windows
to see whether washing them
will make things look better.

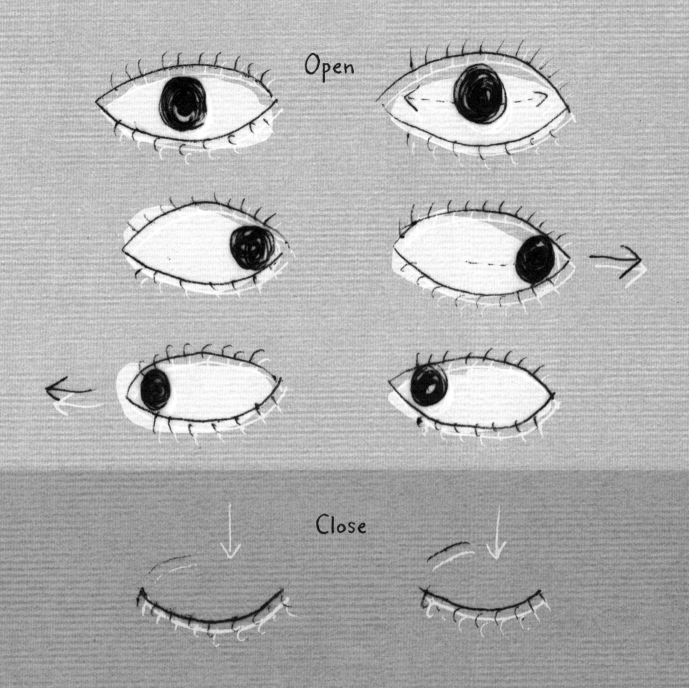

Open

Close

Complain and wash

Between the windows and the pump, there
are two little holes that are tunnels leading
into the Menino.
Air goes in and out through these as fast as
a rabbit can run.

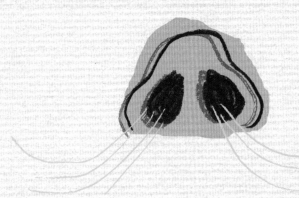

The Menino checks them
frequently and is personally
responsible for keeping
them open.

That's because the Menino loves to breathe.

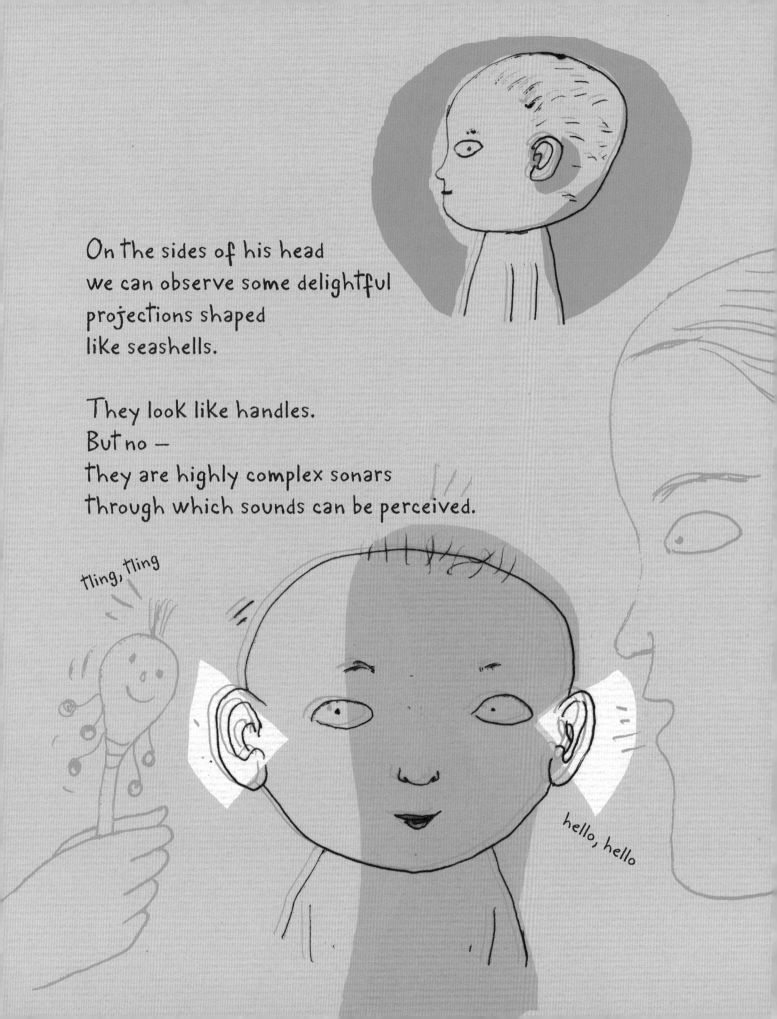

On the sides of his head
we can observe some delightful
projections shaped
like seashells.

They look like handles.
But no —
they are highly complex sonars
through which sounds can be perceived.

tling, tling

hello, hello

The Menino eats
until he is full
and then makes a sound
like a happy toad.

BUURP!

But sometimes he gets all stopped up, and
then the inverse process takes place.

Unfortunately,
you can never tell which of the two
mechanisms will come into play.

The Menino is visited
by the Poop
Fairy Godmother.

She helps him to empty
himself of dirty stuff
and bothersome gases.

She is invisible but
leaves a smelly trace
when passing through.

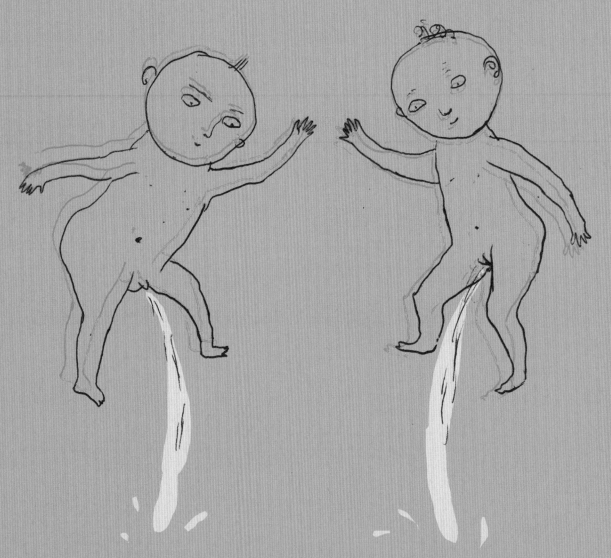

Meninos can also activate a flow of water to
purify themselves.

Each Menino has a fountain.
Some have the "little hole" model
that comes hidden in an elegant fold.
Some have the "little tube" model
that is like a straw with a cushiony base.

For thicker waste, all Meninos have
the same design —
another little hole at the back,
hidden by two lovely meaty bubbles
that also serve as pillows to sit on.

Everything is useful in the Menino.

The Menino illuminates the middle of the night when he turns himself on.

Once, twice, three times...

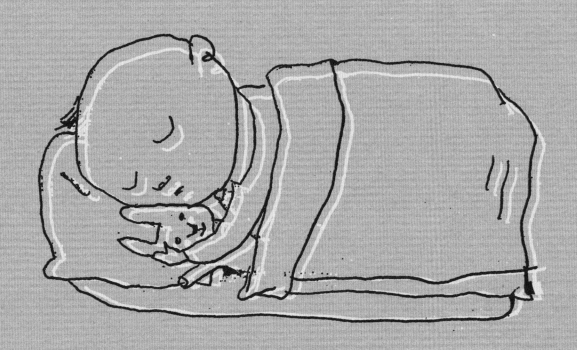

The Menino sets his alarms just in case.
Night is a thief that steals all the colors.

The Menino comes completely articulated.

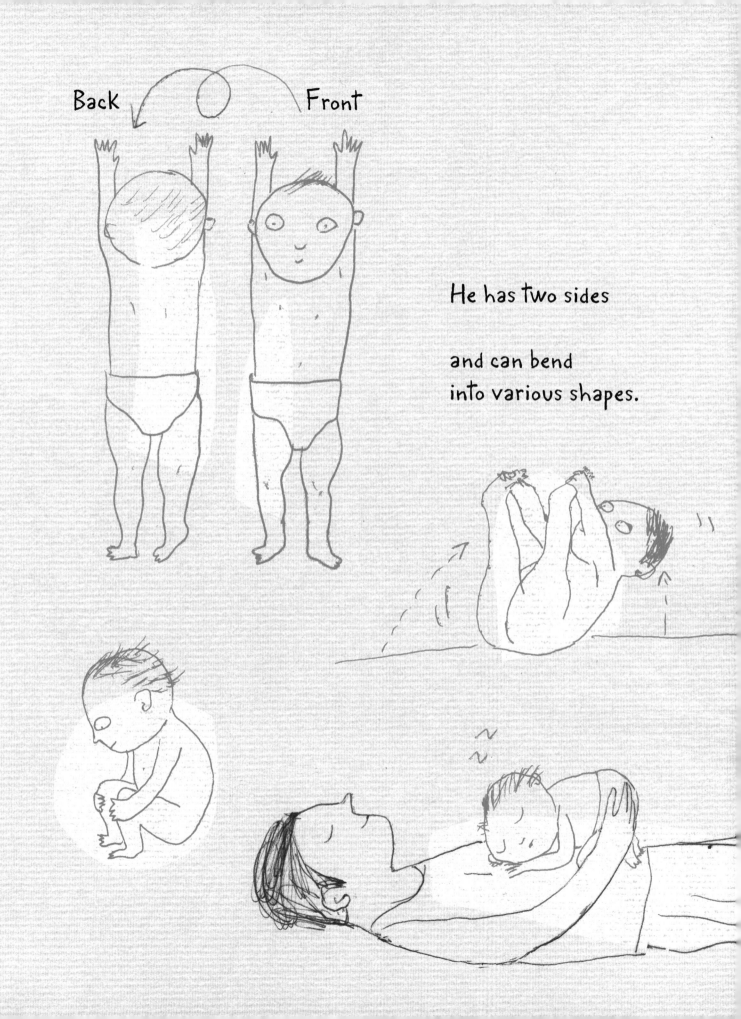

Back   Front

He has two sides

and can bend
into various shapes.

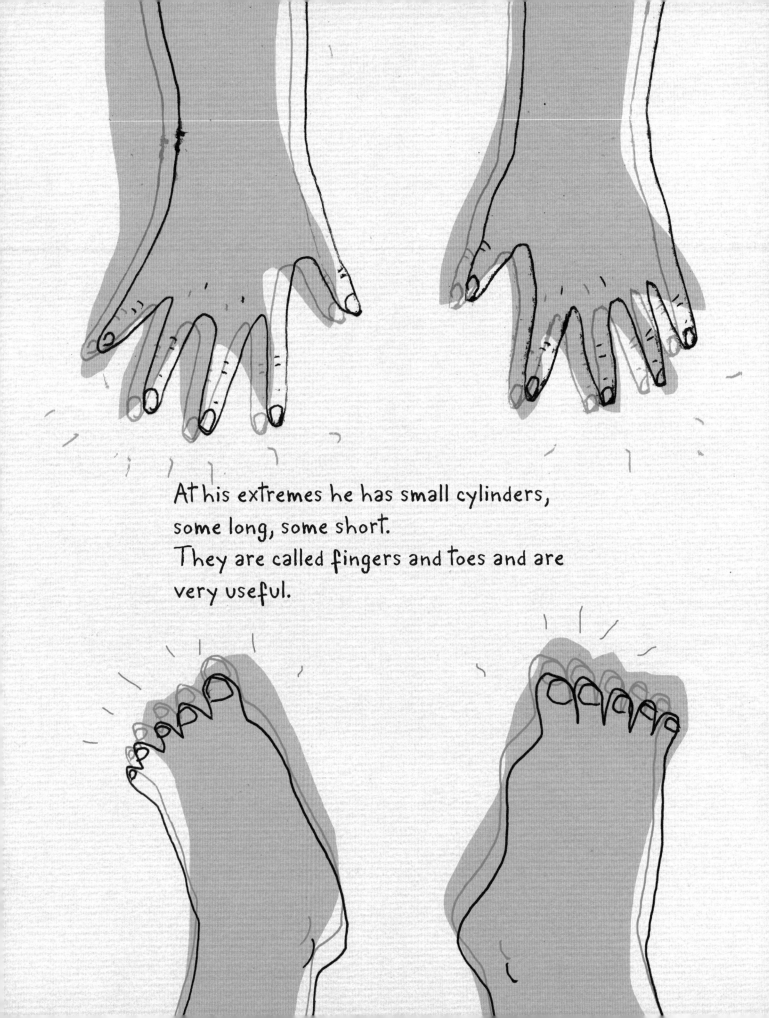

At his extremes he has small cylinders,
some long, some short.
They are called fingers and toes and are
very useful.

But first, the Menino has to master them,
and this takes quite a while.
After all, there are twenty of them and he
has to figure out which does what.

The Menino is always working.

The Menino is mysterious.

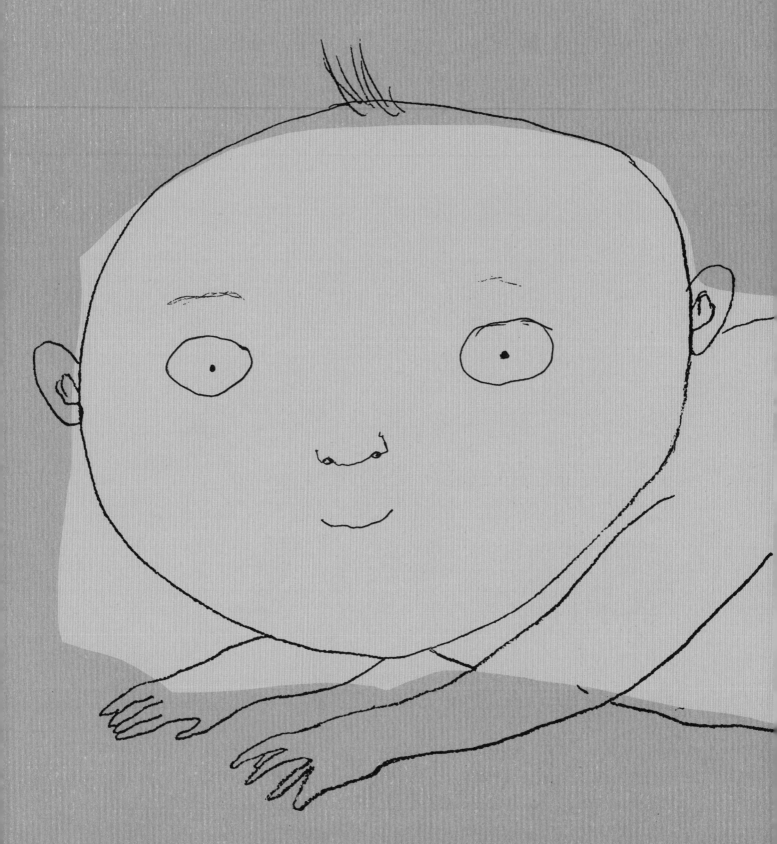

It looks as though he has been blown up like
a balloon through a little knot in the middle of
his body.
But it is so well tied that he never deflates,
although with time he stretches a good deal.
He is made of fantastic material!

There are bald Meninos and hairy Meninos.
There are fat Meninos and skinny Meninos.

The Menino still doesn't know exactly what he looks like.
If he encounters another Menino, he looks at him as though
he were seeing himself. But if he sees himself in the mirror,
he says hi, as though his reflection were another Menino!

At first he doesn't know who is
and who isn't the Menino, but he doesn't worry about it.
All the options seem extremely interesting.

The Menino sees and hears much more than you would think.

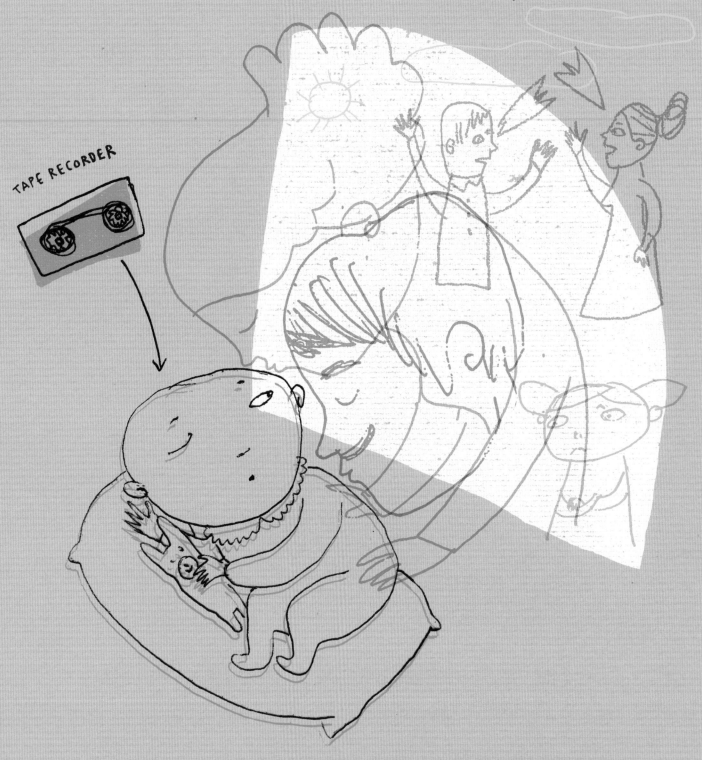

TAPE RECORDER

And he records EVERYTHING in his portable memory.

The Menino is a very successful hypnotist and can cause people to make faces.

If he looks at you and lifts the corners of his mouth like this:

it's impossible not to do the same.

And he can do this trick with large groups of people!

The Menino is also a mirror.

It's useless to try
to pretend in front of him.
It just won't work.

The Menino thinks that if he can't see you,
you can't see him either.

He enjoys being invisible
and having people look for him for a while.

hee-hee

I wonder where
the Menino is.

hee-hee

There you are!

tarrraa

The Menino loves meeting up again.

The Menino has a predilection for small animals.
It's convenient if they are soft and docile.

The Menino wants
to taste everything.

There's no reason to be afraid if one day
some little white stones that weren't there before
appear in his mouth. More than thirty will come out.

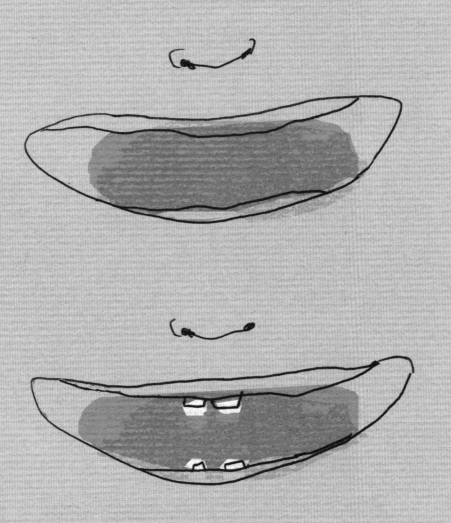

They can hurt the Menino when they are emerging,
but soon he will enjoy cutting and biting very much.
They are also useful for pronouncing the letter "T."

Meninos share a language that
only they understand,
and it is very complicated.

People try to learn it, but it's hard for them.
It just doesn't come out right,
no matter how hard they try.

After a while, the Menino gets
tired of their efforts
and begins to learn the language
that is spoken at his house —
Portuguese, Chinese, English,
Spanish...

waaaa...

He wants water!

It makes things much easier for him.

If when he first arrived, the Menino didn't seem to like the planet so much, slowly but surely he begins to adapt.

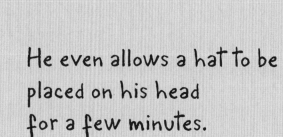

He lets himself be washed with soap
and tolerates people sticking his head and arms
through tight holes.

He even allows a hat to be placed on his head
for a few minutes.

The Menino produces a strange amnesia.
Pretty soon it's hard to remember what life was like
before his arrival. And at the same time, people begin
to remember their own ancient games and songs to
entertain him.

Maybe this is an example of
his hypnotic powers.

It's true that the house is messy
and that it's hard to remember what day
comes after Tuesday.

But the Menino doesn't care about this kind of thing,
and soon enough he convinces people of the same.

And one ordinary day when they are playing with him,
telling him stories or talking in high squeaky voices,
the Menino discovers something surprising...

that big people were
once Meninos themselves.

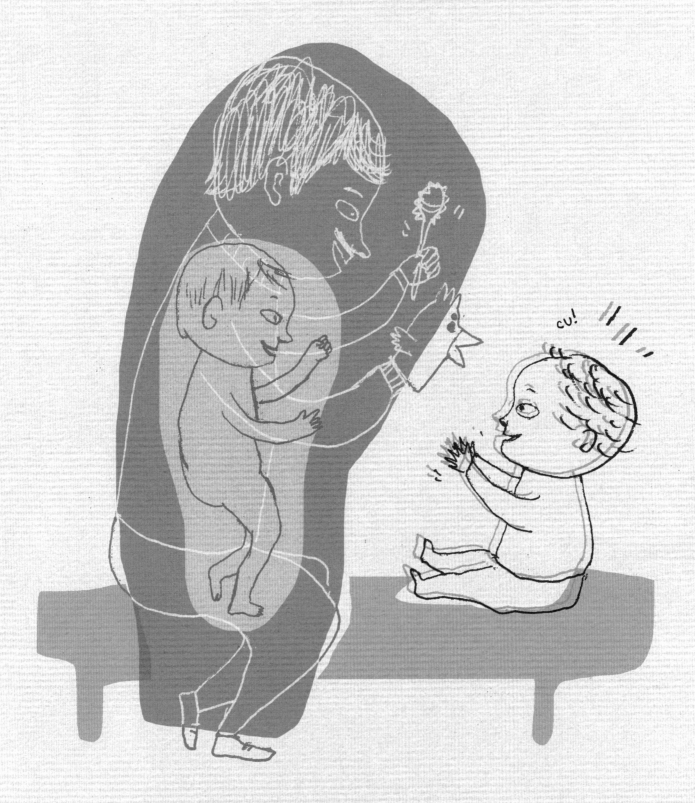

Then the Menino feels
at home...

The End

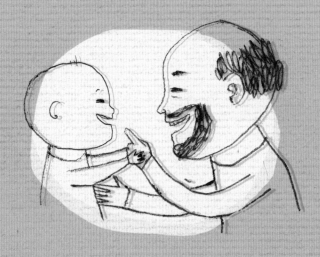

The author when she had
just arrived on the planet.